Disney's TOONTOWN

The Goofed-Up Pet Shop

Written by Margaret Snyder

Illustrated by Jose Cardona and Robin Cuddy

MERRIGOLD PRESS • NEW YORK

oofy locked the door to the Toontown gas station and was headed home when he heard someone calling his name. It was Mr. Fuzzle, who owned the pet shop on the corner.

"Goofy, I need your help," Mr. Fuzzle said. "Would you watch my shop while I deliver this puppy to its new home?"

"Watch the pet shop!" Goofy shouted with excitement. "A-hyuck! Sure, Mr. Fuzzle."

"You won't have to worry about customers because we're closed now," Mr. Fuzzle explained as they hurried to the shop, "but there are a few chores to do."

Mr. Fuzzle quickly opened the door for Goofy. "Okay, Goofy, all you have to do is talk to the parrot, walk the dog, groom the cat, and hop with the frog. I'll be back as soon as I can."

"Don't you worry about a thing, Mr. Fuzzle!" Goofy called.

Mr. Fuzzle tucked the puppy under his arm and rushed down the street.

"Hmmm. Let's see, now," said Goofy as he closed the door. "Something about a parrot and a dog."

"A-hyuck!" he cried at last. "Now I remember. Walk the parrot, then talk to the dog."

Goofy opened the parrot's cage and invited her out. "Come on, now. Time to walk the parrot!" he said.

The parrot tilted her head. "Walk the parrot," Goofy repeated, walking back and forth. "Walk the parrot!" Slowly the parrot followed Goofy around the room. Happily she began to squawk, "Walk the parrot! Walk the parrot!"

"Okay," Goofy said to the parrot, "you keep walking while I talk to the dog."

Goofy picked the dog up out of his cage at the front of the shop. "Howdy, there, little fella. Name's Goofy. Nice to meet ya," he said politely. The dog cocked his head at Goofy. "Let me tell you all about running a gas station," Goofy said. Then he talked and talked about pumping gas, fixing flat tires, and changing oil. The dog barked after everything Goofy said. "Okay, little fella, it's your turn," said Goofy when he ran out of things to say.

While the parrot walked and the dog barked, Goofy tried to remember the rest of Mr. Fuzzle's directions.

"Now I remember! Walk the parrot. Talk to the dog. Hop with the cat. Groom the frog!" Goofy shouted happily.

Goofy scooped up the cat from her place behind the counter and set her down on the floor. "Okay, let's hop!" he said.

The cat didn't move. "Don't be shy," Goofy said, getting down on all fours and hopping around. The cat stared at Goofy. Then she began to hop and meow with glee.

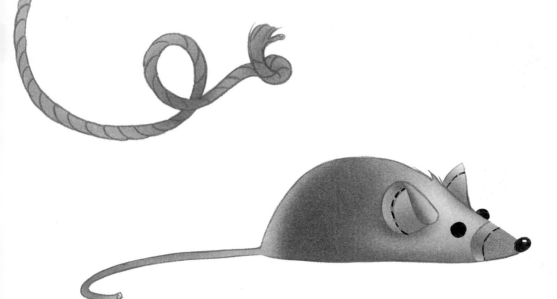

"Now, the frog!" said Goofy. He took the frog
out of his tank. "So, how do you suppose you
groom a frog?" Goofy asked.

The frog just blinked.

Goofy stroked the frog's skin with a soft white
cloth. The frog closed his eyes and began to croak.

"A-hyuck!" chuckled Goofy.

SHAMPOO

Just then Mr. Fuzzle came back. "Oh! Oh, my! What's going on in here?" he asked.

"Ah, well," said Goofy. "I did just as you said, Mr. Fuzzle. I walked the parrot and talked to the dog. Then I hopped with the cat and groomed the frog."

"But, Goofy!" Mr. Fuzzle cried. "I said to *talk* to the parrot and *walk* the dog, and to *groom* the cat and *hop* with the frog!"

"You did?" said Goofy. "Gawrsh, I'm real sorry, Mr. Fuzzle."

Mr. Fuzzle looked around the pet shop. The parrot was happy. The dog was happy. The cat was happy and the frog was happy. In fact, the animals had never been happier.

"Nothing to be sorry about, Goofy!" Mr. Fuzzle said. "As a matter of fact, thanks!" Goofy was confused. Mr. Fuzzle put his arm around him. "Well, my pets have never been happier. So from now on, I'm going to walk the parrot and talk to the dog, hop with the cat and groom the frog. Why, I might even walk the cat and hop with the dog, groom the parrot and talk with the frog." Goofy beamed with pride. It was so nice to help out.